CONKER

First published in Great Britain 1987
This edition published 2002
by Egmont UK Limited
Text copyright © Michael Morpurgo 1987
Illustrations copyright © Gerry Turley 1998
The author and the illustrator have asserted their moral rights
ISBN 978 14052 0257 2
10 9
A CIP catalogue record for this title
is available from the British Library
Printed and bound in the U.A.E

Michael Morpurgo

C·NKER

Illustrated by Gerry Turley

 **YELLOW BANANAS**

Chapter One

MOST DOGS HAVE one name, but Pooch had three – one after the other. Pooch was what Grandma called him in the first place. But when Nick was a toddler he couldn't say Pooch very well and so Pooch soon became Pooh.

Then one day Pooh heard the rattle of the milk bottles outside and came bounding out of the house to say hello to the milkman – he liked the milkman. But today it was a different one. Pooh prowled around him sniffing at the bottom of his trousers. The new milkman went as white as his milk. Nick tried to drag Pooh

back into the house, but he wouldn't come.

''S'like a wolf,' said the milkman, putting his hands on his head and backing down the path. 'You ought to chain it up.'

'Not a wolf,' Nick said. 'He's an old station.'

'A what?' said the milkman.

'An old station,' Nick said. 'Pooh is an old station.' At that moment Grandma came to the door.

'Nick gets his words muddled sometimes,' she said. 'He's only little. I think he means an *Alsatian*, don't you, dear? Old Station! Old Station! You are a funny boy, Nick.' And she laughed so much that she nearly cried. So from that day Pooh was called Old Station.

There were always just the three of them in the house. Nick had lived with Grandma for as long as he could remember. She looked after Nick, and Old Station looked after them both.

3

Everywhere they went Old Station went with them. 'Don't know what we'd do without him,' Grandma would say.

All his life Old Station had been like a big brother to Nick. Nick was nine years old now. He had watched Old Station grow old as he grew up. The old dog moved slowly these days, and when he got up in the morning to go outside you could see it was a real effort. He would spend most of the day asleep in his basket, dreaming his dreams.

Nick watched him that morning as he ate his cornflakes before he went off to school. It was the last day before half-term. Old Station was growling in his sleep as he often did and his whiskers were twitching.

'He's chasing cats in his dreams,' said Grandma. 'Hurry up, Nick, else you'll be late.' She gave him his satchel and packed lunch, and Nick called out 'Goodbye' to Old Station and ran off down the road.

It was a windy autumn morning with the leaves

falling all around him. Before he got to school he caught twenty-six of them in mid-air and that was more than he'd ever caught before. By the end of the day the leaves were piled as high as his ankles in the gutters, and Nick scuffled through them on the way back home, thinking of all the bike rides he could go on now that half-term had begun.

Old Station wasn't there to meet him at the door as he sometimes was, and Grandma wasn't in the kitchen cooking tea as she usually was. Old Station wasn't in his basket either.

Nick found Grandma in the back garden, taking the washing off the line. 'Nice windy day. Wanted to leave the washing out as long as possible,' she said from behind the sheet. 'I'll get your tea in a minute, dear.'

'Where's Old Station?' Nick said. 'He's not in his basket.'

Grandma didn't reply, not at first anyway; and when she did Nick wished she never had done.

'He had to go,' Grandma said simply, and she walked past him without even looking at him.

'Go where?' Nick asked, 'What do you mean? Where's he gone to?'

Grandma put the washing down on the kitchen table and sat down heavily in the chair. Nick could see then that she'd been crying, and he knew that Old Station was dead.

'The Vet said he was suffering,' she said, looking up at him. 'We couldn't have him suffering, could we? It had to be done. That's all there is to it. Just a pinprick it was, dear, and then he went off to sleep. Nice and peaceful.'

'He's dead then,' Nick said.

Grandma nodded. 'I buried him outside in the garden by the wall. It's what was best for him, Nick,' she said. 'You know that don't you?' Nick nodded and they cried quietly together.

After tea Grandma put Old Station's basket out in the shed and showed Nick where she had buried him. 'We'll plant something over him, shall we, dear?' she said. 'A rose perhaps, so we won't forget him.'

Chapter Two

THE DAY AFTER Old Station died was Saturday.
Saturdays and Sundays in the conker season
meant conkers in Jubilee Park with his friends,
but Nick didn't feel like seeing anyone, not that
day. Every time he looked out of the
kitchen window into the back
garden he felt like crying. It was
Grandma's idea that he should go
for a long ride, and so he did.
The next best thing in the world
after Old Station was the bike
Grandma had given him on his

11

birthday. It was shining royal blue with three-speed gears, a bell, a front light and everything. Just to sit on it made him feel happy. By the time he got back from his ride he felt a lot better.

The next morning Nick went off to Jubilee Park as he always did on a Sunday. All his friends were there, and so was Stevie Rooster. Stevie Rooster called himself the 'Conker King of Jubilee Park'. He was one of those bragging brutish boys who could hit harder, run faster and shout louder than anyone else. There was only one thing Stevie had ever been frightened of, and that was Old Station. Perhaps it was because of Old Station that Nick was the one boy he had never bullied.

Of course they all knew about Old Station, but no one said anything about him, except for Stevie Rooster. 'So that smelly old dog of yours kicked the bucket at last,' he said. Perhaps he was expecting everyone to laugh, but no one did.

Nick tried to stop himself from crying.

Stevie went on, "'Bout time if you ask me.'

In his fury Nick tore the conker out of Stevie Rooster's hand and hurled it into the pond.

'That's my twenty-fiver,' Stevie bellowed, and he lashed out at Nick with his fist, catching him in the mouth.

Nick looked at the blood on the back of his hand and flew at Stevie's throat like an alley cat. In the end Nick was left with a split lip, a black eye and a torn shirt. He was lucky to get away with just that. If the Park Keeper had not come along when he did it might have been a lot worse.

Grandma shook her head as she bathed his face in the kitchen. 'What does it matter what Stevie Rooster says about Old Station?' she said. 'Look what he's done to you. Look at your face.'

'I had to get him,' Nick said.

'But you didn't, did you? I mean he's bigger than you isn't he? He's twice your size and nasty with it. If you want to beat him, you've got to use your head. It's the only way.'

'What do you mean, Grandma?' Nick asked. 'What else could I do?'

'Conkers,' said Grandma. Didn't you tell me once that he likes to call himself the "Conker King of Jubilee Park"?'

'Yes.'

'Well then,' said Grandma. 'You've got to knock him off his throne, haven't you?'

'But how?'

'You've got to beat him at conkers,' she said. 'And I'm going to teach you how. There's nothing I don't know about conkers, Nick, nothing. You'll see.'

Chapter Three

SOMEHOW NICK HAD never thought of his Grandma as a conker expert.

'First we must find the right conkers,' she said. 'And there's only one place to find a champion conker and that's from the old conker tree out by Cotter's Yard. It's still standing, I saw it from the bus only the other day. I never had a conker off that tree that let me down. Always hard as nails they are. Mustn't be any bigger than my thumbnail. Small and hard is what we're after.'

And so it was that Nick found himself that

afternoon cycling along the road out of town, past the football ground and the gasworks, with a packet of jelly babies in his pocket. 'Now don't eat them all at once, dear,' Grandma had told him. 'Go carefully and look for the tree on the left-hand side of the road just as you come to Cotter's Yard; you know, the scrapyard where they crunch up old cars. You can't miss it.'

And Grandma's conker tree was just where she said it was, a great towering conker tree standing on its own by the scrapyard.

Nick must have spent half an hour searching through the leaves under the tree, but he couldn't find a single conker. He was about to give up and go home when he spotted a cluster of prickly green balls lying in the long grass on the other side of the fence. There was no sign of life in Cotter's Yard. No one would be there on a Sunday afternoon. No one would mind if he went in just to pick up conkers. There was nothing wrong with that, he thought.

He climbed quickly. At the top he swung his legs over and dropped down easily on the other side. He found the cluster of three small conkers and broke them open. Each one was shining brown and perfect, and just the right size. He stuffed them into his pocket and was just about to climb out again when he heard from somewhere behind him in Cotter's Yard, the distant howling of a dog. His first thought was to scramble up over the fence and escape, but then the howling stopped and the dog began to whine and whimper and yelp. It was a cry for help which Nick could not ignore.

Cotter's Yard was a maze of twisted rusting wrecks. The muddy tracks through it were littered with car tyres. Great piles of cars towered all about him now as he picked his way round the potholes. And all the while the pitiful howling echoed louder around him. He was getting closer.

He found the guard dog sitting by a hut in the centre of the Yard. He was chained by the neck to a metal stake, and he was shivering so much that his teeth were rattling. The chain was twisted over his back and wrapped around his back legs so that he could not move. 'Doesn't look ferocious,' Nick thought, 'but you never know.' And he walked slowly around the guard dog at a safe distance.

22

And then Nick noticed the dog's face. It was as
if Old Station had come back from the grave and
was looking up at him. He had the same gentle
brown eyes, the same way of holding his head
on one side when he was thinking. Old Station
liked jelly babies, Nick thought. Perhaps
this one will. One by one the dog
took them gently out of Nick's
hand, chewed them,
swallowed them and then
waited for the next one.

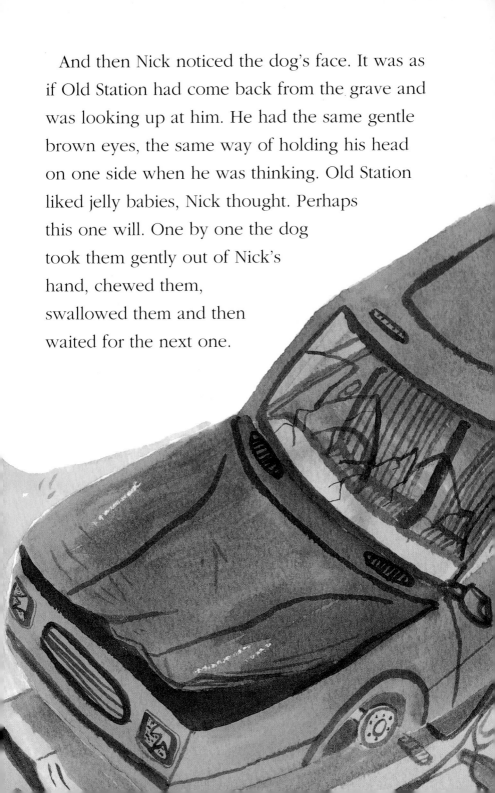

When there were no more Nick gave him the paper bag to play with whilst he freed him from the chain. He ate the bag too, and when he stood up and shook himself, Nick could see that he was thin like a greyhound is thin. There were sores around his neck behind his ears where his collar had rubbed him raw.

Nick sat down beside him, took off his duffel coat and rubbed him and rubbed him until his teeth stopped chattering. He didn't like to leave him, but it was getting dark. 'Don't worry,' Nick said, walking away. The dog followed him to the end of his chain. 'I'll be back,' he said. 'I promise I will.' Nick knew now exactly what he wanted to do, but he had no idea at all how he was going to do it.

It was dark by the time Nick got home and Grandma was not pleased with him. 'Where have you been? I was worried sick about you,' she said, taking off his coat and shaking it out.

'The conkers were difficult to find, Grandma,' Nick said, but he said no more.

Grandma was pleased with the conkers though. 'Just like they always were,' she said, turning them over in her hands. 'Unbreakable little beauties.' And then Grandma began what she called her 'conker magic'. First she put them in the oven for exactly twelve minutes. Then she took them out and dropped them still hot into a pudding basin full of her conker potion: a mixture of vinegar, salt, mustard and a teaspoon

1. Vinegar

2. Salt

of Worcester Sauce. One hour later she took
them out again and put them back into the oven
for another twelve minutes. When they came
out they were dull and crinkled. She polished
them with furniture polish till they shone again.
Then she drove a small brass nail through the
conkers one after the other and examined each
one carefully. She put two of them aside and
held up the third in triumph.

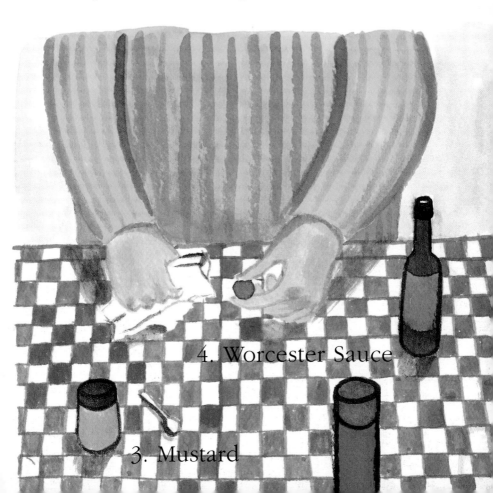

4. Worcester Sauce

3. Mustard

'This is the one,' she said. 'This is your champion conker. All you have to do now, Nick, is sleep with that down the bottom of your bed tonight and tomorrow you'll be "Conker King of Jubilee Park".'

But Nick couldn't sleep that night. He lay there thinking of the dog he had left behind in Cotter's Yard, and about how he was going to rescue him. By breakfast the next morning he was still not sure how to set about it.

'Remember, you must play on a short

string,' Grandma was saying. 'And always play on grass so it won't break if he pulls it out of your hand. And try not to get tangled up - puts a strain on the knot. What's the matter with you, dear? You're not eating your breakfast.'

'Grandma,' Nick said, 'what if you found a dog all chained up and lonely and miserable, would you try to rescue it?'

'What makes you ask a thing like that, dear?' Grandma said.

'Would you?' Nick asked.

'Of course, dear.'

'Even if it meant stealing it, Grandma?'

'Ah well, that's different. Two wrongs don't make a right, Nick,' she said. 'What's all this about?'

'Oh nothing, nothing,' Nick said quickly. 'I was just thinking, that's all.'

Nick could feel she was suspicious. He had said far too much already. He left quickly before she could ask any more questions.

'Good luck, Nick,' Grandma called after him as he went off down the path.

He cycled right up to Stevie Rooster in the
Park and challenged him there and then. 'I've
got a conker that'll beat any conker you've got,'
he said. Stevie Rooster laughed at Nick and his
little conker, but when his first conker broke in
two the smile left his face. He took conker after
conker out of his sack, and each one was
shattered into little pieces within seconds. A

crowd gathered as
Nick's conker became a twentier,
a thirtier, a fiftier and then at last an eighty-fiver.
Stevie Rooster's face was red with fury as he
took his last conker out of his sack.

'Your turn,' Nick said quietly and he held up
his conker. There still wasn't a mark on it. Stevie
swung again and was left holding a piece of

empty string with a knot swinging at the end of it. Nick looked him in the face and saw the tears of humiliation start into his eyes. 'You shouldn't have said that about Old Station,' Nick said and he turned, got on his bike and cycled off leaving a stunned crowd behind him.

Chapter Four

IT WAS A twenty minute ride up to Cotter's Yard, but Nick did it in ten. All through the conker game he had been thinking about it and now at last he knew what to do. He had a plan. He was breathless by the time he got there. The gates were wide open. The Yard was working today, the great crane swinging out over the crushing machine, a car hanging from its jaws.

'Hey you, what're you after?' It was a voice from the door of the hut. It belonged to a weasel-faced man with mean little eyes.

'I've come to buy your dog,' Nick said. 'Haven't got any money, but I'll swop my bike for your dog. It's almost new, three speed and everything. Had it for my birthday, a month ago.' Nick looked around for the dog, but there was no sign of him. The chain lay curled up in the mud by the hut.

'Haven't got no dog here,' said the weasel-faced man, 'not any more. Wasn't any use anyway. Got rid of him, didn't I?'

'What do you mean?' Nick said.

'Just what I said. I got rid of him. Vet came and took him away this morning. No use to me he

wasn't. Now push off out of here.' And he
went back inside the hut and slammed the
door behind him.

As Nick cycled home, the rain
came spitting down through the trees.
He had never felt more miserable in
his life. When Old Station died he
had been sad enough, but this
was different and much, much
worse. This had been his
fault. If only he had come
back earlier, if only. By
the time he reached
home he was blinded
with tears.

'Well, and how's the "Conker King of Jubilee Park"?' Grandma called out from the kitchen as he closed the door behind him, and she came hurrying out to meet him. 'Well I told you, didn't I? I told you. It's all down the street. Everyone knows my Nick's the Conker King. Well, come on, let's see the famous conker. An eighty-fiver, isn't it?'

'Eighty-sixer,' Nick said and burst into tears against her apron.

'What's all this?' Grandma said, putting her arm round him and leading him into the kitchen. 'We can't have the "Conker King of Jubilee Park" crying his eyes out.' And Nick blurted it all out, all about Cotter's Yard and the poor starving dog he had found there that looked just like Old Station, about how the vet had come and taken him away.

'I was going to buy him for you with my bike,' Nick said, 'to take Old Station's place, but I was too late.'

'Who says you were?' said Grandma, and there was a certain tone in her voice.

'What do you mean?' Nick asked.

'What I mean, dear, is that if you'd wipe your eyes and look over in the corner there, you'd see a basket with a dog in it, and if you looked hard at that dog you might just recognise him.'

Nick looked. The dog from Cotter's Yard lay curled up in Old Station's basket, his great brown eyes gazing up at him. The dog got up, stretched, yawned and came over to him.

'But how . . . ?' Nick began.

Grandma held up her hand.

'When you came home from Cotter's Yard yesterday with your duffel coat stinking of dog, I was a little suspicious. You see, old Cotter's known for the cruel way he looks after his guard dogs, always has been. And then when you asked me this morning if I would rescue a dog if I found him all chained up and hungry and miserable - well, I put two and two together.'

'But he said the Vet came and took him away - he told me,' Nick said. 'So he did, dear, so he did. We went out there together, the vet and me, and we made old Cotter an offer he couldn't refuse. Either we took his dog with us or we reported him for cruelty to animals. Didn't take him long to make up his mind, I can tell you.'

'So he's ours then, Grandma?' Nick said.

'Yours, Nick, he's yours. Old Station was mine. I had him even before I had you, remember? But this one's yours, your prize for winning the Conker Championship of Jubilee Park. Now can I see that famous conker or can't I?'

Nick fished the conker out of his pocket and held it up by the string. Before he knew it, the dog had jumped up and jerked it out of his hand. A few seconds later all that was left was a mass of wet crumbs and chewed string.

'It looks as if he likes conkers for his tea,' Grandma said.

'Better call him "Conker" then,' Nick said. And so they did.

Yellow Bananas

Yellow Bananas are bright, funny, brilliantly imaginative stories written by some of today's top writers. All the books are beautifully illustrated in full colour.

So if you've enjoyed this story, why not pick another from the bunch?

Author	Title	ISBN
KEVIN CROSSLEY-HOLLAND	Storm	07497 4698 X
MALACHY DOYLE	Long Grey Norris	14052 0594 6
ANNE FINE	Design a Pram	14052 0113 7
ANNE FINE	Countdown	07497 4672 6
ANNE FINE	Scaredy Cat	14052 0251 3
JAMILA GAVIN	Deadly Friend	14052 0113 9
JAMILA GAVIN	Fine Feathered Friend	07497 4224 0
ROSE IMPEY	Who's a Clever Girl, Then?	14052 0480 X
PENELOPE LIVELY	Dragon Trouble	14052 0132 0
MICHAEL MORPURGO	Conker	14052 0257 2
MICHAEL MORPURGO	Colly's Barn	14052 0255 6
MICHAEL MORPURGO	Snakes and Ladders	14052 0134 7
JACQUELINE WILSON	My Brother Bernadette	07497 4223 2